CW01582372

The Goddess's Wishes

Lissette E. Manning

To Lindsay,
Enjoy the book.
Thanks for your support.
Lissette E. Manning

The Goddess's Wishes

The Child of Calamity Series

Book 1

Copyright © September 2013 Lissette E. Manning

Published © September 2013 L.D.B. Press

ISBN-13: 978-0615813875 (paperback)

All rights reserved.

The author retains sole copyright to her contributions to this book.

No part of this publication may be reproduced, stored in a retrieval system, or transmitted in any form or by any means, electronic, mechanical, photocopying, recording, or otherwise, without prior written permission of the publisher.

For information and inquiries, please address, Nancy Medina, via the following email address: lizziebeth1095@sbcglobal.net.

This book is a work of fiction and any similarities to any persons, living or dead, or places, events, or locales, is purely coincidental. The characters are productions of the author's imagination and used fictitiously.

ADVANCE READER'S COPY

•

NOT FOR SALE

This is an advance reader's copy from an uncorrected proof. These pages have been set for this edition only, and do not reflect the type, design, or layout to be used in the final edition. Readers are reminded that changes may be made in this proof copy before the book is printed. If any material from the book is to be quoted in a review, the quotation should be checked against the final bound book. Dates, prices, and manufacturing details are subject to change or cancellation without notice.

Please note that books will not be available for purchase until the release date has been specified by the publisher. All reviews should be scheduled to run after that date has been set.

We'd love to hear what you think.

Please forward all emails to the following address:
LizzieBeth1095@sbcglobal.net.

For more information about the author's books, please visit her website:
http://www.simplistik.org

This version of this book serves as an **Advanced Reader's Copy.**

This **Advanced Reader's Copy/You** are subject to the condition that it shall not, by way of trade or otherwise, be shared, sold, duplicated, modified, hired out, or otherwise circulated without the **Author's** or the **Publisher's**, (**whichever one has shared the book with you forthwith**), prior written consent in any shape or form of book binding or cover, (**be it print or ebook**), other than that in which it is published, and without similar condition, including this condition being imposed on the subsequent **Purchaser/Reader**.

This copy is strictly confidential. It may not be used in any shape or form other than the way in which it was specified between **party** and the **Author or Publisher**.

Violators of this agreement are subject to, but not limited to, civil or criminal action and monetary damages.

To Maya.

TABLE OF CONTENTS

AUTHOR'S NOTE:

Fair warning, Lovelies.

I've taken a little literary license with the Greek gods and goddesses. I thought I should mention this, because several relationships throughout the series itself are not cannon. Some find themselves in situations they normally wouldn't, and I've tweaked their usual details to suit the purpose of the stories/series itself.

For example, while Artemis might be known as one of the chaste virgin goddesses, she's anything but chaste. She does things to suit her purposes, and has a voracious appetite/attitude to match. She has an agenda to fulfill, and will do everything possible to make sure things are done to her specifications.

I apologize in advance for the literary license I've taken with the characters and their purported histories. I do hope none of you mind me doing so. After all, anything is possible when writing fiction, right?

Lissette E. Manning

ACKNOWLEDGMENTS

To Joel, thank you for always lending me your eyes and ears, as well as the suggestions/insight you give me on occasion whenever I need it. You've come to mean a lot to me. I truly value your friendship, and hope we'll always endure whatever comes our way. I can't wait to see things take flight for you some day soon with your own writing, Sweetness. Much love and hugs from me to you!

To Sharon, you get a mention here, as always, because I couldn't do this without you. I appreciate everything you've done for me – your thoughts, suggestions, tweaks, and everything else. Best of wishes always on your own journey. May it bring you happiness and more!

To my sister, Mary. I know we don't always see to eye to eye, but I truly do treasure you. Whatever you need, Chica, I'm there. You're missed more than you know. Que Dios te bendiga siempre, hermana mia. A dondequiera que estes, alli estoy contigo en espiritu. Te quiero mucho!

To my fans/readers, you all make this journey quite worthwhile. I hope you enjoy the book very much.

CHAPTER 1

Artemis materialized in the middle of her brother, Apollo's, bedroom with a resounding pop. A smile of satisfaction spread across her lips as she watched him scramble out of bed in search of his clothes. A look of annoyance clouded the features of the demi-goddess lying on his bed, clutching the bed sheets tightly to her chest.

Her silvery-yellow eyes narrowed as she stared at the demi-goddess, Dyina, and pointed to the adjacent door. "Get out!"

"Damn it, Artemis!" Apollo growled as he tugged his chiton into place. "Can't you knock?"

Artemis grinned, and made her way toward the chaise lounge tucked into the left corner of the room.

"Where's the fun in that, brother?" she quipped, lowering her slender frame onto the settee.

The demi-goddess rummaged about the room for her clothes, her blue eyes sending imaginary vicious daggers in Artemis' direction. The goddess's smile never faltered as she watched her brother and his current paramour move about the room. Apollo took a moment to show Dyina to the door, his shoulders taut with tension as he swung the door closed.

"I'm assuming you're here for a favor of some kind?" Apollo asked, running a hand through his thick blond curls.

"Something like that."

He approached the table nearby, and poured himself a glass of red wine. He knocked back his drink in one gulp, and promptly poured himself another before taking a seat in the chair in front of the lounge she reclined on.

"What now?"

She bestowed him with a knowing gaze, her lips quivering with effort as she tried to hold back her excitement. "I want Mount Olympus, brother, and you're going to help me get it."

He snorted with amusement, and downed the glass

of wine. "A lofty goal, Sis, but that's not likely."

Her smile disappeared, her eyes narrowing to half slits. "I expected more from you."

He summoned the pitcher of wine, and filled his glass once more. "Do you honestly think dear old Dad is going to give up the throne so easily?"

"No, but that's where you come in. He owes us. Besides, we've always been his favorites."

"Whether he owes us or not, Artemis, you'll never get him to step down."

"Not yet, but I will. And when I do, Mount Olympus will be mine!"

Apollo tossed his head back, and laughed heartily. "So you think. There's a good many of us with an eye on Daddy's throne. You're not likely to get it, nor are any of us."

Her nostrils flared outward with anger as she stared at her twin brother. "You owe me."

"I'll pay up. Eventually."

She sat up straight, staring deep into her brother's eyes. "You'll pay up now, brother dear. Zeus has been careless, and I intend to unmask him before the other gods and goddesses."

"How, pray tell?"

A photograph materialized in thin air as she flicked her hand about. He deftly caught the glossy paper between his fingers, and examined it.

"Who is she?"

"I suspect she's one of Daddy's illegitimate children. The one the prophecy speaks of."

His lips pursed with concentration. "Prophecy?"

She nodded. "Yes. The *Child of Calamity*, Apollo. I think she's the one."

Apollo wracked his brains as he did his best to remember the prophecy she spoke of. Unfortunately, nothing came to mind.

"She doesn't look like anything special. She looks like she's completely mortal."

"Appearances can be deceiving."

"I know, but I still think she's harmless. How old is she anyway?"

"She's nineteen, and she lives in New York."

"New York? Really?"

"Yes. Her mother's certainly striking, so I can sort of understand what Zeus sees in her."

His brow furrowed as he examined the photograph

once more. "What does this have to do with me?"

She smiled, her eyes shining with delight. "You're going to fetch her for me."

"Me?" he sputtered with disbelief.

"Yes. You're the perfect candidate, Apollo," she breathed as she shifted her position, and leaned closer to him. Her lips hovered above his own. "You're hard to resist."

The picture fluttered to the floor as Apollo's stormy blue gaze fell upon her mouth. "If that is so, then why do you resist me on occasion?"

She frowned, and pulled herself out of his reach. "You're my brother!" she mumbled as she pushed herself to her feet, and strode toward the open window.

He followed suit, and wrapped his arms around her. He brushed his lips along the curve of her neck, playfully nipping at her flesh. "That's never stopped you before."

"Damn it, Apollo!" she grated, and disengaged herself from his embrace. "Not now. We've other matters to attend to."

He snorted with derision. "Attend away!"

Her heart hammered within her chest as she stared at him. She wanted very much to give in to what she was feeling, but she knew she couldn't. Not now, anyway. If she was to succeed in having her plans fall through, she needed to be strong. Falling prey to her baser desires right now would not bode well.

Squaring her shoulders, she promptly replied, "You need to find her, and bring her to me."

Apollo's mouth thinned to a tight line. "You could make that happen with a flick of your hand, Artemis. I honestly don't see why you need me to do your dirty work."

"You are the *God of Light*, brother, and the sun itself. You see and hear everything. You've a better chance in finding her than any of us combined."

"For someone who's known as the chaste huntress, you sure as hell don't make use of that damned title! You're supposed to be a protector, of sorts, too. Yet here you are entreating me to hunt a woman you deem to be the *Child of Calamity*. That's a massive contradiction, don't you think?"

She crossed her arms about her chest, her chin rising with determination. "If you won't help me, Apollo, then I'll get someone else to do it."

"I never said I didn't want to."

"Yeah? Well, you sure as hell are acting like you are. Think of the power we could garner by working together. If we take out the one thing he loves the most, then Daddy dearest won't know what hit him. This woman is the one the prophecy speaks of. I'm sure of it. Why else would she be so well protected?"

Apollo frowned. "How come I've never seen her before?"

"You never pay attention to things unless it's really necessary. You obviously prefer your trivial pursuits over the needs of the court, thus you've no true knowledge of what goes on here on Mount Olympus."

"That's not true!" he balked.

"It is, and you know it."

Displeasure flickered across his face. "You know what? Get someone else to do your dirty work!" he replied haughtily, and orbed himself out of the room.

Artemis stared at the spot he'd been standing in, moments ago, with dismay. She'd wanted her brother's help in more ways than one. Deep inside, she'd assumed he'd be easy to bring over to her side. Unfortunately, she'd been mistaken on that account. An idea soon popped into her head. She smiled, her silvery-yellow eyes gleaming with ruthless cunning.

No matter, she thought. *I've other ways to make things happen.*

With one last look about her brother's room, she dematerialized, intent on putting her plans into motion, one way or another.

CHAPTER 2

"Is there a reason you've decided to set foot into my realm, Artemis? It better be important!" Hades barked as he tossed a stack of papers across his desk.

She smiled broadly as she popped up near a dais her uncle had placed in front of the fireplace. "It is," she assured, tossing her auburn hair over her left shoulder.

He quirked an eyebrow in her direction, and crossed his arms about his chest. "Oh?"

She pursed her lips, running her fingers across the dais's soft fabric. "I need you to help me find someone."

Hades' eyes narrowed with suspicion. "For?"

Artemis' heart thumped rapidly within her chest as she realized she'd come to the wrong person for help. "A long-lost family member."

He snorted with amusement. "Did you really think I'd fall for that?" he quipped, and dropped his six-foot-two frame onto his chair. "I know each and every member of our family, Artemis. Some quite personally, so whatever claims you were going to make are invalid."

"You don't know about this one. Nobody does. I came across her by accident. Daddy dearest has kept her well hidden."

"You've been trailing one of Zeus' offspring?"

"Yes. I doubt you've an idea as to whom I speak of, though."

"You have proof?"

"Of?"

"That she was sired by Zeus."

"Some."

He settled back against his chair, and produced a pitcher of wine in front of him. The decanter floated gently onto the desk. A goblet appeared in the air, fluttering toward him. He caught the glass in mid-air, and poured himself a glass, waiting for her to continue.

"I'm waiting."

"For what?"

"Proof."

She presented him with perfect pout. "You won't take my word for it, Uncle?"

He knocked back his drink in one gulp, and shook his head. "No. I know you, Artemis. Your hunting comes with unwanted benefits. I'm not sure as to what you want this person for, but it can't be good."

"I'm curious about her, that's all."

"I beg to differ."

She growled with frustration, and snapped her fingers together. The photograph she'd shown Apollo, moments ago, floated in his direction. He plucked the piece of paper out of the thin air, and scanned the picture. A muscle jumped across his jaw as he gazed upon the young woman's face.

"Where did you get this?"

She shrugged nonchalantly. "Deivos brought it to me."

"How did he come across this?"

"I don't know."

His nostrils flared outward with anger. "Yes, you do."

She shook her head with vehemence. "No, I don't.

He wouldn't tell me. I've tried everything I know to try to make him talk. Trust me on that."

Hades smirked with amusement. "I'm surprised your feminine wiles didn't work to your advantage."

"He's a demi-god, Uncle. Not all demi-gods fall under my spell," she replied haughtily.

"Where is he now?"

"New York, I gather."

"Bring him to me."

An appalled expression spread across her face. "I'll do no such thing!"

He tossed the photograph aside. "Then expect no help from me."

"But . . ."

"None, Artemis. Have I made myself clear?"

She clenched her teeth together in order to keep herself from verbally lashing out at him. "Yes, Uncle."

He nodded, and flicked his hand at her in dismissal. "You may go."

She kept her silvery-yellow eyes pinned on him. Without another word, she orbed herself out of Tartarus. She'd lost yet another consort, but she wasn't out for the count. At least, not yet. There were a good many whose services she could employ to do her bidding. She just needed to find the right person for the job. With a knowing smile playing about her lips, she sped off to Mount Olympus, hopeful that she'd find someone to follow through on her requests soon enough.

CHAPTER 3

A startled cry was rent from Artemis' lips as she strode into her room. Her half-brother, Hermes, lay across her bed, his shrewd gaze centered on her face. She gathered her composure, and held her head high as she walked further into her chambers.

"What are you doing here?" she asked as she made her way over to the washing basin.

Hermes examined his fingernails, a knowing smile upon his lips. "Our dear brother mentioned that you might need me."

Her eyes narrowed with suspicion as she glanced at him over her right shoulder. "Oh?"

"Apollo wasn't wrong, was he?"

She turned away from him, and grabbed a small scrap of cloth resting next the basin. She dipped it in the lukewarm water, and wrung the excess water out. Normally, she left such trivial tasks to her servants, but she wasn't in the mood to deal with their attentions. She knew her servants meant well, but sometimes, she found their presence quite cumbersome. Most especially when they fawned over her repeatedly.

"What did he tell you?" she asked as she ran the cloth across her collarbone.

"Not much, actually. Just that you required my assistance."

She snorted with amusement. "Why would he think that?"

He shrugged, and pushed himself off of the bed. "You tell me."

She drew the cloth across the expanse of her shoulders, uncaring about the fact that the peplos she wore was getting wet. Hermes approached, and pulled the washcloth out of her grasp, dropping it into the basin. He turned her around, and clasped her chin between a thumb and forefinger, gently pulling her head up.

"What's going on, Artemis?"

She bit her lip, wondering as to whether she could trust him. Though he'd done her bidding many times in the past, there was no telling how he'd take the news that she was plotting to overtake the throne. He and Zeus got along well, she knew, and she was well aware of just how tight his relationship with her father was. Should she take one wrong step, he was likely to betray her at a moment's notice.

She pulled her chin free of his hold, and offered him a smile. "Nothing, brother. Apollo and I had a disagreement, that's all."

"About?"

"This and that," she replied airily.

He frowned. "Are you sure?"

She nodded. "Yes."

Hermes unclasped the pouch strapped around his waist, and dug within its depths. He found what he was looking for, and held a piece of paper aloft in her direction. Her heart pounded inside her chest as she stared at his offering.

"What's that?"

"Take it."

She was hesitant to do so. "Why?"

He stormed toward her, and dropped the paper into her hands. She looked down, and realized that the parchment wasn't just a piece of paper. The very photograph she'd shown Apollo not too long ago lay in her hands. How her brother had gotten a hold of a copy of it, she did not know. Yet the fact that he had spoke volumes. He might have been angry with her, but he was still willing to assist her with her plans. That thought alone pleased her.

"Do you know who she is?"

"No, but I'm of the mind to find out."

"Apollo mentioned something about the prophecy concerning the *Child of Calamity*."

On guard, she rose to her full height. "What exactly did he say?"

"Not much, actually. He asked me as to what I knew of it. I tried to explain, but he seemed way too distracted. It was almost time for the sun to crest over the Earth to signal a new day, so he wasn't that forthcoming about what he wanted. He had time enough to hint that you needed help, however."

Her taut stance relaxed. She made her way to the table, scrumptious food spread across its entire surface.

Plucking several green grapes off of a plate, she tossed the succulent orbs into her mouth. "I see."

"Are you going to tell me what you're up to?"

She glanced in his direction as she poured herself a cup of wine. "What I need, dear brother, requires complete secrecy. Not even Zeus must know."

His mouth thinned to a tight line. "You're not planning to incite Father's wrath, are you?"

She feigned a look of abject horror. "God, no!" she balked, and downed three more grapes.

Hermes did not look convinced. "You are, aren't you?"

"Do I look as if I'd do such a thing?"

He wrapped his arms around his chest, staring down at her with displeasure. "You have in the past," he pointed out.

"That was then, Hermes. I was young and carefree. I didn't know any better. Besides, Daddy dearest has forgiven me for my past indiscretions."

He rolled his eyes at her, not quite taking her words at face value. "You might look innocent and demure, Sister, but we all know you're not. You're up to something."

She nonchalantly waved a hand through the air in hopes of shrugging off the sense of unease that threatened to overcome her. She was strong and independent. Willful, at times, too. Yet she'd never cowered before anyone aside from her father. If she was to succeed in accomplishing her current goals, she needed to remember that.

"I'm not," she lied, her tone deceptively sweet. "I just want to know who this woman is. She's tied to us somehow, Hermes, and I want to know why. I want to know if she's a threat to our existence."

He dropped his tall frame onto the nearest chair, his lips pursed. "You honestly believe she's family?"

"Yes. Why else would she be so well guarded?"

He shrugged. "She's human, Artemis. There's a good many reasons as to why her caretakers protect her so thoroughly. Perhaps you're putting too much into things? There's a possibility she's not even what you think she is," he reasoned.

Her jaw tightened with frustration. "I'm never wrong, brother."

"That's debatable."

"What does that mean?"

"Your passion has clouded your judgment on occasion. Yes, you're strong and decisive. You're able to maintain your calm whenever possible, but you often lose yourself to the emotions running through you, allowing yourself to falter when you should not. I think this is one of those times. This woman seems harmless. She's nothing you should worry about."

Anger burned in the depths of her eyes. Hermes was right, but she would not admit it to him. She would not allow him to point out more of her flaws at whim. Nor would she buckle beneath the onslaught of his words. She knew, then, that his assistance was one she could do without. Though he was a formidable adversary, his allegiance to their father was apparent. Should she take one wrong step, he'd thwart her plans in an instant.

A cold mask settled upon her face as she calmly replied, "You know what, you're right."

"I am?"

She nodded. "Yes. I shouldn't soil my hands with such trivial matters. I'm obviously mistaken. You said it yourself; she's nothing but a human. Mortals are beneath us, right?"

He sat up straight, a weary expression upon his face.

"Yes, they are," he agreed. "This insignificant creature doesn't deserve our attention. You should set your sights on something more important."

"Like what?"

He grinned, his blue eyes shining with mischief. He spread his arms wide. "We're on Mount Olympus. Food, drink, and countless days of debauchery are our lofty goals. Set aside your worries, Sister. Enjoy the life you've at your fingertips!"

A corner of her mouth lifted with amusement. "I shall!" she said, turning her attention back to the food sitting on the table. "Now, if you don't mind, get out."

His smile faltered. "You're serious?"

She looked at him out of the corner of her eye, tossing a piece of cold venison into her mouth. "Yes. Get out."

His mouth tightened, and his nostrils flared with anger. Without another word, he disappeared, leaving her to her own devices.

She sighed with relief, and dropped into the chair behind her. She listlessly picked at the plate of food in front of her, her mind reeling with the implications of what she and her half-brother had discussed. She knew

Hermes wouldn't keep quiet for long. He'd find a way to know more about the girl in the photograph. She was sure of it.

She needed to keep him from doing so, and soon. He'd ruin her carefully constructed plans otherwise. The question was, how could she do so without soiling her hands further in the process?

CHAPTER 4

"A penny for your thoughts?" Poseidon inquired as he sat down on the bench next to Artemis.

She looked up with surprise. "Uncle!"

He chuckled softly, his blue-green eyes roving across the expanse of the immaculately kept garden spreading out before them. "You rarely venture out this way, my dearest niece. Is something wrong?"

She nibbled on her lower lip in thought, basking in the peace and quiet the garden offered those who tread within its depths. "No," she said a tad too quickly.

"Artemis . . ."

She looked down, picking at the folds of her peplos's skirt with the edge of her fingernails. "It's just the usual. I worry about those under my care. The animals and the young women I present myself to. People seem distracted these days, and barely offer us thanks for the blessings we bestow upon them."

He regarded her through veiled eyes. "Are you sure that's it?"

She nodded absently. "Yes."

"Why do I think otherwise?"

She'd forgotten how perceptive her uncle truly was. At seven-feet-six inches tall, he exuded an aura of strength and masculinity that rivaled no other. He used his charm and swarthy good looks to his advantage. Women, and men, fell at his feet whenever they lay eyes on him. She often wondered if he enjoyed such attention, or whether he got bored of being revered quite so often.

"It's nothing."

He reached out to clasp her hand, patting it gently. "You can trust me."

She kept her eyes focused on the lush green grass below her feet. "Can I?"

"Have I ever failed you?"

"No."

"But?"

She looked up at him, and frowned. "Hmmm?"

"There's an unspoken *but* hovering in the air."

She snorted with amusement. She'd forgotten how easily her uncle could pull her out of her sulking moods. "Sort of."

"So . . ."

Artemis gazed into the depths of her uncle's eyes, wondering if she could truly trust him. Her consorts in finding the *Child of Calamity* had failed her, thus far, and part of her was afraid to seek out the help of one of the higher gods or goddesses. Common sense told her that it wouldn't hurt to ask him for his opinion on the matter. Though, she knew she ran the risk of losing everything she'd strived for in the process.

"I've been looking for someone," she said, moments later.

"Anyone I know?"

"I'm not sure."

"Is this person here on Mount Olympus?"

"No."

His eyes focused on her slumped form. "Who?"

"A mortal."

"A mortal?"

"Yes. A woman, to be exact."

He sat back against the bench, and crossed his arms about his chest. "You've never been one to be so fixated on lesser beings. What's changed?"

She turned to face him, her silvery-yellow eyes narrowed slightly. "I need to know I can trust you."

"Artemis . . ."

"If I'm to tell you what I know, I have to be sure that you won't throw me to the wolves."

His jaw clenched tight. "I wouldn't."

"Yes, you would. You've betrayed people in the past, Uncle. Mostly when it suits you in order to gain the upper hand, but still . . ."

He sighed, and pinched the bridge of his nose between a thumb and forefinger. "I've done things I'm not proud of. I admit it, but when it comes to those I love, I do my best to protect them. Except Zeus. He can rot in Tartarus for all I care."

She chuckled, and shook her head. Unbidden, tears pricked her eyes. "And you'd protect me?"

"If it came to that."

Her mouth trembled as she fought to retain her composure. "I want to believe that."

His heart constricted as he noticed the bright sheen of moisture shining in her eyes. "You should. Now, tell me about this woman. Why does she vex you so?"

"She doesn't vex me. Not exactly. It's what she represents that draws me to her."

"And?"

She bit her lip once more. "I believe she's the *Child of Calamity*."

His eyes opened wide. "The *Harbinger of Chaos and Destruction*?"

"Yes."

"How did you come by this knowledge? Do you know what she looks like?"

Her heart hammered within her chest as she saw the calculating look in his eyes. "I . . . My source is irrelevant."

"Unless you tell me exactly what I need to know, I can't help you, Artemis."

"If I'm to divulge said information, I require a favor in return."

Poseidon stood up, looking down at his niece in contemplation. She was up to something. He could sense it. Whenever something or someone caught her attention, it led to consequences that were usually out of her control. She had a knack for both getting into trouble and inciting it. Artemis might look sweet and virginal, but she was nothing like what she portrayed herself to be. She was cold, cunning, and quick to the cut.

"And what favor would that be?"

She pushed herself to her feet, gliding toward the stone wall nearby. She pressed her hands against it, her mind working hard to come up with a plan that would benefit her in the long run. Poseidon would make a formidable consort, she realized. He detested Zeus' ruling far more than any of the other gods and goddesses. If she were to bring him completely to her side, she'd be able to use his talents to her advantage whenever possible. Though, she needed to be careful to not divulge more than what was necessary in order to keep her uncle from knowing about her exact plans for Mount Olympus.

"I'll get back to you on that."

"You do that. I'll be waiting to hear from you soon. Whatever you're up to, Artemis, it does not bode well. Be careful with what you do. You wouldn't want to make enemies of those who are willing to support you."

With that, he disappeared. Her heart raced as she

stared at the horizon. Poseidon knew she wasn't being truthful with him. He would not remain passive in the situation at hand. He, too, would search for the *Child of Calamity*. She knew she couldn't allow him to find her. She would make it possible for Artemis to bring her father to his knees. The throne would be hers, one way or another. No one would take it from her.

CHAPTER 5

Artemis' mind wandered as she walked down the halls of her home on Mount Olympus. Servants hurried about preparing a feast in honor of her return, as well as making sure that everything was spic-and-span. Her handmaidens trudged at her heels, eager to catch her up on the goings-on inside the home. While she was grateful for their company, and enjoyed their exuberance immensely, she found their presence a tad cumbersome at that given moment.

She dismissed them, and continued on to her bedroom, intent on taking a warm, calming bath. Pushing the door closed behind her, she strode toward the bathroom, pulling off her clothes as she moved along. A smile of delight crossed her face as she eyed the large tub of hot, steaming water standing before her.

She added several drops of rose oil to the water, mixed it in with a flick of her hand, and promptly stepped into the tub. A sigh of pleasure and relief slid past her lips as she leaned back, and comfortably settled into the water. She kept her eyes closed, and allowed her hands to roam across her breasts.

A frisson of awareness rippled through her as she pinched her nipples between her thumbs and forefingers. Her breath grew ragged as her body came to life. Sliding her right hand downward, she lightly trailed her fingertips across her navel toward her aching mound. She slipped a finger past her pink folds, rubbing her clit ever so gently.

She spread her legs wide, allowing the water's heat to amplify the warmth gathering at the tender juncture of her thighs. With a quick flick of her hand, her fingers slipped inside, her muscles clenching tight around the slick digits. Working the appendages back and forth, she moaned aloud as she allowed herself to climax.

Basking in the afterglow of her orgasm, she was not aware of the unexpected presence inhabiting her bathroom. Her eyes flew open with surprise as the water began to bubble around her, coaxing another orgasm from her depths. Apollo stood before her in all of his naked splendor. Her heart hammered within her chest as she stared up at him with surprise.

"What are you doing here?" she asked as he stepped into the tub.

A knowing smile played about his lips as he saw her clamp her legs together. He rubbed his aching cock, keeping his eyes on hers.

"I wish to pleasure you," he said, reaching out to wrap his hands around her knees.

She cursed the tub's limited mobility as he shoved her thighs apart, intent on sliding between them. In the blink of an eye, she found herself wrapped in a towel on the other side of her room. Apollo glared at her, upset that she'd thwarted his attempt in gaining satisfaction.

"That's not necessary," she said, as she clutched the towel tightly to her.

"You mean to leave me unsatisfied?"

"You have a multitude of chits at your disposal. Surely, you do not need me?"

He stood up, and stepped out the bathing tub, water coursing down his muscular body as he moved toward her. "They are not you, Artemis. None know how to pleasure me the way you do."

Her eyes closed of their own volition as he reached out, and curled a hand around her cheek. Her body ached for fulfillment, but she knew it had to be denied. She pulled herself out of his grasp, and strode toward the wardrobe where all of her clothes were kept. She selected a dress made of the finest silk, and allowed the towel to drop to the floor.

She tugged the fabric over her head, and carefully pulled it into place. Next, she drew forth a pair of dainty red slippers, and slipped her feet into them. Approaching her vanity table, she sat down, and grabbed her hair brush, running it through her auburn tresses. All the while, she tried to ignore her brother's imposing presence.

Apollo snapped his fingers together, and manifested a white chiton with a yellow sash upon his tall frame. Brown leather sandals encompassed his large feet. He made his way over to her, and settled his hands upon her shoulders. Their gazes clashed as they stared at one another through the vanity's mirror.

"Deny it all you want, Sister," he breathed, "but your

body craves for what I can give you."

She snorted with amusement, and turned her attention back toward brushing her hair. "What is it you really want, Apollo? I've no time for games today."

He reached out, and clasped her hand, gently bringing it behind her back to press her fingers against his aching member. "I told you, satisfaction."

Her breath quickened, her eyes dark with wanting. The thought of satisfying her baser desires was tempting. God knows, she needed a little release herself, yet she knew she couldn't fulfill his request. At least, not yet. She had more pressing matters to attend to, and now was not the time for her to impale herself on a man's cock, much less on Apollo's.

He sensed her arousal, and leaned forward to brush a hand across her bare left shoulder. He slipped his fingers beneath the edge of her dress, and moved it downward to cup her breast in the palm of his hand. He raked his nails across her nipple, his penis throbbing painfully. Letting go of her arm, he brought his free hand upward to curl his fingers around her chin. He tilted her head back, and bent his head to catch her lips with his. She moaned, allowing him access into her mouth. His tongue plundered its warm depths as his hand plucked and pinched her taut nipple.

Artemis caught herself before he could go any further. She shoved her chair back, causing him to release her and step aside. She pushed herself to her feet, and pulled her clothes back into place. Ignoring her body's hunger, she left Apollo standing in place, and promptly teleported herself out of her chambers without another word.

CHAPTER 6

"Artemis?" Deivos inquired as he came face-to-face with the beautiful goddess.

She smiled, and stepped out of the shadows, her silvery-yellow eyes appraising his six-foot-seven frame. "Deivos," she breathed. "How good to see you!"

His eyes narrowed as he took in her seductively clad body. Her auburn hair was loosely curled around her shoulders, fluttering gently in the soft breeze. She now wore a pair of tight black leather pants tucked into thigh-high black leather heeled boots along with a black sheer blouse. Beneath it, a black and red corset hugged her flesh, her ample breasts peeking over its top edge. Gold and silver bracelets clinked around her wrists, and she wore a diamond ring on each of her ring fingers. A gold belt completed the look, hanging low around her waist.

"Gettin' ready to party, eh?"

She chuckled softly, and shook her head. "No. I've come to see you, actually."

His hazel eyes widened with surprise. "Dressed like that?"

Her smile disappeared. "What's wrong with what I'm wearing?"

"N – Nothin'. It's just . . . Ya don't look like yer dressed for a casual chat, Love. In fact, I 'onestly thought ya were 'eaded to a club or somethin'."

"Oh. Well, no. I'm just here to see you. I was in the mood to feel beautiful and seductive, that's all."

He clasped her hand, and led her over to a settee sitting in the middle of the room. "Well, ya 'ave certainly achieved 'at. 'Ave a seat. Is there anythin' I can get ya?"

She waved her hand about. "I'm fine, thanks. Sit down, Deivos. We need to talk."

A frowned marred the beautiful contours of his face. He slid into the leather recliner across from her, prepared for the worst. "What about?"

"Have you found out who she is?"

"Who?"

"The girl in the photograph you gave me. Several weeks have passed since you first gave me that photograph, and I've heard nothing else from you. I held off on taking further action because I figured you were hard at work in finding out what I wanted to know. Is that not the case?"

He breathed a sigh of relief. "It . . . Yes, 'at's the case. I've been 'ard at work, yes."

She raised a brow at him in question. "Well?"

"'Er name is Callidora Spiros."

"*Gift of Beauty*," she mused. "Anything else?"

"No, Milady. All I was able to discover was 'er name. An' 'at was only 'cause I came across 'er at a club the other night. She's quite talkative once she's 'ad a couple drinks under 'er belt."

Artemis frowned. "That's it? All this time, and all you have to show for it is her name? Did you at least think of following her?"

He lowered his eyes as he felt his face grow warm. "I tried."

"But?"

"It's like she disappeared. She got wind of the fact 'at

someone was followin' 'er. One minute, she was there, an' the next, she was gone."

Her jaw clenched with effort as she fought to hold back the anger boiling beneath the surface. "Have you seen her since?"

"No. But –"

She raised a hand, and cut him off. "Enough! I expect results, Deivos. If you're to share in the spoils of war, you have to be more efficient."

His head snapped up with surprise. "Spoils of war? Is she 'at important?"

She leaned forward, exposing her ample cleavage to his view. "Of course, she is. Why else would I have you find out more about her?"

He fidgeted uncomfortably, adjusting his pants as they tightened across his crotch. "I assumed she was just a passin' fancy of yers."

She smirked, and shook her head. "Hardly. I'm the protector of young girls, Deivos. Her safety has been in question ever since you brought her to my attention."

He swallowed audibly as his face paled. "Someone's after 'er?"

"Yes, and I want to make sure no harm comes to

her," she lied smoothly. "Which is why you have to work harder in finding out everything you can about her. Where she lives, who she stays with, and what she does during the day or night. Anything and everything about her must be accounted for. Is that understood?"

He withered beneath her intense scrutiny. "Yes, Milady. I will do my best."

She stood, smoothing out the imaginary wrinkles on her sheer blouse. "You do that," she replied, and orbed herself out of his living room, leaving him alone to contemplate as to whether their conversation had ever happened in the first place.

CHAPTER 7

A myriad of thoughts spun through Artemis' mind as she walked along Sixth Avenue. She'd given Deivos the task of finding out everything possible about Callidora Spiros, but her curiosity in regards to the girl would not let up. Thus, she'd done a little digging of her own, and had come across the address leading to the girl's work place.

She stopped in front of the small boutique, and pretended to window shop, discreetly taking a look inside. A raven-haired beauty lounged against a counter, her cornflower blue eyes focused on something Artemis couldn't see. She surmised that young woman was approximately the same height as she, five-feet-eight inches tall. Though, she could have been wrong, as the girl was wearing a pair of black stilettos.

She was tempted to march inside, and pluck the chit out of the store in order to take her back to Mount Olympus. Yet she knew she couldn't. Without the proper information at her disposal, there was no telling as to whether her current prey really was the *Child of Calamity*. Though the prophecies spoke avidly of the *Harbinger of Chaos and Destruction*, there was no mention of what the child looked like. Nor would anyone know as to whom the being in question would be born to. All she had were her assumptions. Yet deep inside, she knew the girl was tied to the pantheon itself. She just didn't know how. Not yet, anyway.

A sharp gasp broke past her lips as she turned around, and bumped into the last person she expected to see. "Hades!"

He smiled down at her, his dark-brown eyes shining with amusement. "Beautiful, isn't it?"

"What is?"

He pointed to the dress in the window. "The dress. You should try it on."

She turned around to assess what he was looking at.

Where moments ago there hadn't been anything, a silvery-yellow strapless dress adorned a delicate-looking mannequin. She gasped with astonishment as she saw the dress take on a different form before her very eyes.

Gold and green leaves spread across the bodice's border, inching toward its seam, and down to its hem. Interspersed with the leaves, she saw images of a huntress holding a bow and arrow as numerous animals crowded around her. The ivy moved upward, and came to a stop at the V-shape holding the bodice and flared skirt together. The dress was beautiful, and she found herself wanting it all the more.

"Y – You did that!?"

Hades grinned. "Of course. Go on in. Try it on."

"But . . ."

"You know you want to, so I'm giving you the opportunity you seek. Consider this a gift, though it comes with a warning. The girl must not come to harm. None. At all. Is that understood?"

She frowned. "How did you . . . ?"

His eyes gleamed with suppressed menace. "I have my ways. You're not the only one searching for answers, Artemis. You must hurry. Time is of the essence, so make use of it!"

He disappeared, leaving her alone. Several passersby stared at her with perplexion as she mumbled to herself. She ignored their curious looks, and cursed her uncle for being so astute. She should have known that he'd dig further into the situation at hand. The fact that he'd deduced what her next course of action might have been also disturbed her. Yet she chose not to think about that fact for the time being. Gathering a hold of her composure, she took a deep breath, and strode into the shop.

***

"May I help you?" Callidora Spiros inquired as Artemis stepped inside.

She plastered a timid smile upon her lips, and nodded. "Yes," she said, her voice a tad breathless. She pointed to the dress Hades had fashioned for her as it sat in the adjacent window. "I'd like that dress."

Callidora's gaze swung toward the mannequin she was now pointing to. "You've good taste. That dress is made by Herbert Underland."

Artemis stifled a laugh, and feigned ignorance. *I'm so going to give my uncle hell about that later!* "Who?"

Callidora rolled her eyes, and waved her hand about in dismissal. "You're kidding, right?"

"Umm . . . no."

She walked over to the mannequin, and gently tugged it down. "Herbert Underland is THE man of the hour. His fashion designs are found all over the world. As you can see, he uses the finest silks. The embroidery is to die for!"

Callidora spoke as if she'd known about Hades her entire life, yet Artemis knew such a fact was impossible. Most especially since her uncle had created the garment at a moment's notice.

No, she thought. *Hades must have placed such thoughts in her head in order to make the dress's creation more credible.*

The girl plucked the dress off of the mannequin, and held it up to the light. "Sadly, his creations are expensive as hell."

"You own some?"

"Gosh, no. I wish."

Artemis' gaze was drawn to the garment once more. "It's a beautiful dress. Quite exquisite, if I may say so."

Callidora smiled softly, and ran her finger along the dress's seam. "Yes, it is. The careful craftsmanship he employs on each item he makes is amazing."

Goodness, Uncle. Was it really necessary to alter her mind so much? she thought.

Keeping her thoughts in check, she said, "I've never seen such fashion before, in all honesty."

"You should check him out on the internet. He's got a lot of stuff available. Most are already ready-to-wear."

The internet? Dear God, what is that?

"Umm . . . yeah. Sure."

"The color of the dress seems to suit you. It matches the color of your eyes."

Artemis smiled, her silvery-yellow eyes gleaming. "It would look great on you, too," she commented casually. "You've the body for it."

A small smile danced across Callidora's lips. "It is beautiful, but . . ."

"But . . . ?"

She sighed dramatically. "I can't afford a dress like."

Artemis assessed her from head to toe. She wore designer clothes and shoes, exuding an air of refinement. It was obvious she was properly bred, yet she was working at a station that seemed quite beneath her.

Odd, she thought.

"Is it really that expensive?"

Callidora nodded. "A bit."

"I think I'll take it anyway."

"You won't regret it," Callidora replied, slipping the dress into Artemis' waiting hands.

Artemis glanced down at the delicate fabric, admiring her uncle's handiwork. The dress was beautiful. Hades had given her the means in which to meet Callidora. She was grateful to him for giving her the opportunity, yet she could not deny that he didn't trust in her completely. Though, he didn't know it, the girl was a vital part of her plans. She'd gain a small foothold in the scheme of things if she were able to bring the girl onto her team. The question was, how was she going to do that if she barely knew the young woman to begin with?

Clearing her mind, she followed Callidora over to the cash register, and produced a wallet with a quick flick of her hand. The girl's eyes widened, but she kept quiet as her eyes focused on the money Artemis had stashed within the leather's folds. The goddess pretended to riffle through the wad of cash.

"How much do I owe you?"

Callidora cleared her throat, and glanced down at the register's screen. "Twenty-five hundred."

"That's it?"

"You want it to be more?"

"Well . . . You said this guy's pieces were expensive."

"With the meager earnings I earn, they are."

"Meager earnings? You don't quite fit in here, in all honesty," she murmured offhandedly.

Callidora looked away, avoiding her intense scrutiny. "Yeah, I get that a lot."

Artemis wanted to place a gentle hand on the girl's shoulder, to comfort her somehow. Yet she knew that sort of thing would not be welcome, most especially since she'd just met the girl.

"I see."

A soft sigh escaped Callidora's lips. "Shall I finish ringing you up?"

The bright sheen of moisture in the girl's eyes wasn't lost on Artemis. There was something she was hiding, she was sure of it. Curiosity got the best of her. She wanted to know as much as possible about Callidora, but she tamped the urge to ask questions down. Now was not the time or place for her to indulge in such things.

Instead, she said, "Sure."

She handed over the necessary amount, unaware of the surprised looks in her direction from several customers lounging nearby. Callidora's fingers flew across the register's interface, and she quickly rang up Artemis' purchase. She accepted the bag, change, and receipt once the transaction was complete.

"Thank you," she murmured as she slipped the money and the piece of paper into the left pocket of her tight leather pants. She turned around, intent on leaving, when Callidora's voice reached out to her.

"Thanks for stopping by. I hope you like the dress."

She smiled, her eyes alight with pleasure. Composing herself, she whirled about, and nodded. "I do. Thanks again!"

Without another word, she walked out of the boutique, clutching the paper bag tightly between her fingers. It took every ounce of willpower for her not to turn around, and walk right back to further engage Callidora. With a quick flick of her hand, she sent the bag back to the store with Callidora's name on it, and a note tucked within its depths. She lamented the fact that she wasn't keeping the dress, but she knew the girl's curiosity would get the best of her when the time came. Sooner or later, she would seek Artemis out.

She continued walking, her mind focused on the events that had taken place not too long ago. There was something about the young woman that drew her attention. She wanted to know more about her. To obtain her complete confidence, something she so clearly needed when the time came to gain her acquiescence. One way or another, she would have her allegiance. Only then, would she be able to put her plans into motion, once and for all.

CHAPTER 8

"You seem to be in good spirits," Hades commented as he fell into step beside Artemis.

She smiled. "Yes, and I have you to thank for that, Uncle."

"All went well, then?"

She stopped in her tracks, and turned to face him. "Yes," she said. "Quite well."

He ran a hand through his dark-brown curls, a knowing smirk upon his lips. "That's good, I suppose. You didn't buy the dress, though."

"I did."

He quirked a brow at her in question. "But . . . ?"

She looked down momentarily, and wrung her hands

together. "Callidora admired it, too. I thought it would look better on her since she has the body for it. After our impromptu meeting, I sent it back to the store with a means for her to find it."

Hades stared down the bridge of his nose at her. For a moment, it looked as though he'd crossed his eyes. The intensity of his gaze made her shift uncomfortably. She was tempted to look away, but her pride refused to allow her to do so. If she was to remain strong and self-sufficient, she needed to show everyone around her that she did, indeed, possess those qualities.

"Why do I have a feeling that you didn't do so out of the kindness of your own heart?"

Her eyes widened with mock horror. "How can you say such a thing, Uncle?"

"As I said once before, your hunting comes with unwanted benefits. I'm still not convinced that your interest in this mortal is pure of heart."

Her lips pursed with displeasure. "If that's the case, then why did you help me?"

"Curiosity got the best of me. I want to know why you're drawn to the girl so much."

"And?"

He crossed his arms upon his chest, his head tilted slightly to the side in contemplation. "I'm not a hundred percent sure on that yet. Perhaps you'd like to enlighten me?"

Her pulse raced as she realized he was fishing for answers. Answers she could not give him. Though he was her favorite uncle, she knew he would thwart her plans in a heartbeat. Most especially if he were to know that they involved taking over Mount Olympus. Every god and goddess coveted the golden throne. Many had tried to take it from her father, but none had succeeded in doing so.

She, on the other hand, was determined to make it hers, once and for all. Her duplicity was to be one that no one would see coming. Well, if Apollo made sure to keep his mouth shut, anyway. She still needed to silence him on that account. The question was, how?

The sound of Hades' clearing his throat brought her out of her reverie. "What?" she prodded, a slight frown marring the center of her forehead.

"I'm still curious as to why the girl intrigues you."

"She's family."

"Are you sure?"

"Why wouldn't she be?"

The left corner of Hades' mouth tilted upward with amusement. "Perhaps you should dig a little deeper, and get your facts straight, Artemis. What if she really is a mortal? What then?"

She stared back at him, appalled. "There's no way she could be, Uncle. She's too well-protected."

"Some humans can afford to be. The girl obviously has money, so . . ."

Her frown deepened. She'd noticed Callidora's designer clothes and her air of refinement from the get-go. Yet the girl had tried to play things off as if they were nothing. She was hiding who she was for a reason.

But why? she wondered. *Can it really be so simple?*

She straightened to her full height of five-feet-eight, and focused her silvery-yellow eyes on her uncle. "Why are you really here?"

Hades spread his arms wide, feigning innocence. "I came to see how things went for you. Nothing more."

The hairs on the back of Artemis' neck stood on end. He was purposefully keeping something from her. "What aren't you telling me?"

"Nothing you already know, dear. I just want to

make sure that the girl comes to no harm."

"Why?"

"Let's just say I now have a vested interest in the situation."

"Such as?"

His dark eyes bored into hers. "Such as, I'm keeping my eyes on you. Be careful of where you tread. Not everyone will give you the helping hand you seek."

He disappeared, leaving her alone to ponder his words. She realized, then, that he knew more about the situation than he let on. Deciphering exactly what he knew was another matter entirely, however. He was good at keeping secrets just like she was. If she was to remain one step ahead of him, she needed to know what he knew. To do that, she needed to seek out the one person she never thought of seeing so soon – the beautiful and enigmatic Persephone.

CHAPTER 9

Artemis closed her eyes, and took a breath to steady herself, oblivious of the world around her. In the blink of an eye, she found herself in the middle of Persephone's chambers on Mount Olympus. Unfortunately, she was not alone. Hades was with her. His presence in the room was a stark contrast to his usual place in Tartarus. The pair turned to face her. A knowing look flashed across Hades' face, while annoyance clouded Persephone's delicate features.

"What are you doing here?" Hades inquired as he handed his wife a white silk dress.

"How did you get here so quickly?" Artemis shifted uncomfortably beneath her uncle's sharp gaze.

"I'm a god, Artemis. We travel faster than the speed of light. You know that as well as I do. Is there something you want?"

"I came to see Persephone."

"In regards to?"

"Something."

A glint of menace danced in Hades' eyes. "Such as?"

She airily flicked a hand about. "It's a woman's thing. You wouldn't understand."

"You'd be surprised as to what my husband understands," Persephone said as she accepted the dress he handed her. "Is it dire?"

"Is what dire?"

Persephone assessed her from head to toe, and shook her head. "Your problem. Because if it's not, I don't have time to address it right now."

Artemis' eyes widened as she became cognizant of what Persephone was doing. "You're packing!"

"Yes, I am."

"But . . . Why? You're not due to go back to Tartarus yet."

Her aunt glanced at her husband, and smiled. "I'm heading home several days early."

"Won't that disrupt the balance of seasons?"

"It just means that winter comes a little early this year, that's all. I miss my home, Artemis. Surely, you can understand that?"

"Well, yes, but . . ."

Hades dropped the bundle of clothes he was now holding, and came to stand in front of her. His dark eyes bored into hers. "Why are you really here?"

"I told you, I need to –"

"Talk to my wife, yes. I got that already. About what?"

A muscle twitched along her jaw as Artemis clenched her teeth tight with frustration. "It's personal."

Her uncle chuckled. "I know all about women's ailments, dear. Now don't be shy. Tell us what's wrong."

She stared at him, looking appalled. "N – No!" she cried, and orbed herself out of Persephone's quarters.

She soon found herself in the middle of her own room. Pacing back and forth, she angrily tugged at her auburn curls as she mumbled to herself. Hades must have known she'd seek Persephone out.

But how? she wondered. *How is it that he's one step ahead of me?*

A swift knock upon her door drew her attention. "Who is it?"

"It's Nephele, Milady," the voice replied.

"Yes?"

The doors opened, and a petite blond strode inside. Her hazel eyes swept appreciatively about the room. "Is there something you require?"

"No."

The girl nodded, and turned around, intent on leaving.

"Wait!"

Nephele faced Artemis once more, a look of adoration spreading across her face as she stared at her mistress. "Yes, Mistress?"

Artemis hurried to the desk sitting to the left of her bed, and scrawled a short message across a piece of parchment. She folded it thrice, heated a piece of red wax, and stamped her sigil, a bow and arrow sitting upon a lunar disk, in the middle in order to seal the letter closed. She turned around, and made her way over to her handmaiden. With a flick of her hand, she slipped the parchment into the girl's hands.

"I need you to deliver that to my brother, Apollo."

Nephele glanced at the letter. “Yes, Milady. As you wish.”

A deep frown marred her forehead as she waited for the girl to fulfill her request. Frustration boiled up within her as Nephele remained where she was standing. Minutes passed, and still, she did not move. Instead, her eyes were pinned on Artemis’ taut form.

“Well?”

“Yes, Mistress?”

“Aren’t you going to do as I have asked of you?”

Embarrassed, Nephele glanced at her sandal clad feet. “Must you not dismiss me?”

Artemis’ cheeks flushed a deep red color. “Oh. Yes! You’re dismissed.”

The girl curtsied before her, and hurried toward the open door. She murmured a quick, “Thank you,” as the door swung closed.

A soft sigh slid past her lips as she glanced about the room. Nothing was going as planned. She’d made a small headway in regards to Callidora, but it was not enough to get things to where they needed to be.

She turned on the balls of her feet, and made her way toward the balcony, overlooking the expansive gardens below. She was not yet close to achieving her goals. Though, she was confident everything would come together soon enough. Granted, she'd encountered a bit of opposition, thus far, but none of it had deterred her plans as of yet.

Hades and Apollo's involvement in the scheme of things needed to be addressed. She had to make sure they were both on her side. Apollo, she knew, could be taken care of easily. Hades, on the other hand, was another matter entirely. Never-the-less, she was determined to gain the upper hand, at all cost. The battle for Mount Olympus depended on it.

CHAPTER 10

Knowing that it would be awhile before Apollo made his appearance, Artemis decided to seek a little entertainment. She strode out of her room, and walked down the brightly lit corridor. Her mind was full of turmoil as she thought about the plans she'd set into motion.

She wanted everything to be perfect for when the time came for her to take over the throne. Callidora was one of her father's illegitimate children. She was sure out of it. The woman protecting the girl was certainly beautiful. She wasn't quite sure if she was the girl's real mother, but she'd find out soon enough.

The *Child of Calamity* was an avid part of her plan.

Once her father was made aware of her existence, he'd do everything possible to keep her a secret. Each and every god and goddess coveted the lore behind the prophecy itself. While no one knew the child's gender or name, the thought of having such power at their disposal was something everyone wanted.

Except Zeus. Her father often claimed that the prophecy was a lie. That it was created to ensure that Mount Olympus was ruled with an iron thumb. Yet it is known that behind every lie, there is always a truth. She was convinced she'd found it. Aside from those who were avidly carrying out her wishes, no one truly knew of the child's existence.

Aside from Hades, she mused. *I've a feeling he knows more than he's letting on. Why he's keeping things a secret, I do not know.*

Artemis sauntered into the main courtyard of her home, and came to a complete stop. Deivos sat on a wooden bench beneath her favorite willow tree, his shoulder-length brown hair fluttering softly in the breeze. Her nipples hardened as his hazel eyes roved over her now casually clad body. Her mouth grew dry as their gazes clashed, and she saw the hunger burning in his eyes.

Gathering her composure, she said, "What are you doing here?"

A knowing smile played about the demi-god's lips. "Ya tol' me to keep an eye on the girl."

"Yes, and?"

"I've news."

She crossed her arms upon her ample breasts. "Go on."

"I've found 'er. Where she works, sleeps, who she 'angs wit'."

Artemis chuckled, and flicked her right hand in the air in dismissal. "I found her place of work not too long ago. Though, her home address will come in handy. Have you found out anything in regards to her mother?"

"No."

"Her father? Is it Zeus?"

"I'm not sure."

She frowned. "Then what am I paying you for?

"Payin' me?" he balked. "Ya call romps in my bed payments? Please, 'at's barely scratchin' the itch between my balls. Ya ain't paid me shite, Artemis, an' ya know it."

Her mouth dropped open with surprise. "How dare you . . . ?"

Deivos stood up, pulling himself up to his full height. He towered over her, his eyes glinting with anger. "I dare, Goddess, 'cause I'm tired of bein' ya lackey. 'Ell, I'm tired of bein' your boy-toy, too. I don't mind doin' ya favors if it benefits me, but this shite wit' the girl . . . . It's gettin' old."

She curled her fingers into tight fists, her eyes blazing with fury. "No one," she breathed, "speaks to me like that!"

He snorted with derision. "I'm not afraid of ya, dearest cousin. I've gone through enough shite wit' ya to know when yer jus' 'ot air."

Though she was not prone to using the elements to her advantage, Artemis was determined to teach him a lesson. She gathered the particles of water hovering in the air above as Poseidon had taught her to do, and willed them into a full-blown storm. Water pelted them from every direction, the brunt of the storm centered upon Deivos. Lightning crackled above him as she wove several wards in the air with quick jerks of her hands.

His eyes widened as a lightning bolt struck him dead center in the chest. The electricity passed through him, and was absorbed into the ground. He had no chance of regaining his composure before roots and vines exploded from the ground, pinning his soaked body in place. The wind picked up, whipping his sopping wet hair into his eyes. He roared with anger, pleading with Artemis to cease her attack, but the force of the elements continued to batter him left and right. Whatever she'd done had made his ability to teleport useless.

She grinned broadly as she lifted her hands in front of her, and a small vortex of fire spread between her fingers. She sensed his distress, and saw the horror plastered across his face. The thought of marring his perfect complexion tugged at her heartstrings, but she needed to teach him a lesson. One that would remind him of his place when it came to doing her bidding.

In the blink of an eye, the water, lightning, roots, and vines disappeared before she had a chance of tossing the ball of flame in his direction. She swore with vehemence, and tried to call up the elements once more, but something prevented her from doing so. A quick tap on her shoulder soon drew her attention. Her eyes widened as she whirled around to face her father.

"What are you doin'?" he asked, his stormy blue eyes narrowed slightly.

Her chin rose with determination. "Having a lover's spat, Daddy dearest."

"Since when do you use the elements with such abandonment? I didn't show you how to use my lightnin' bolts 'at way." He looked toward Deivos, and nodded. "You may go."

"But I'm not finished with him!"

"You are now," Zeus replied as his nephew regained his powers, and teleported to safety. "Seriously, girl, what are you thinkin'? What would Demeter think if she were to have seen you abuse the earth in such a manner? Poseidon would be appalled to see you use his precious water with such careless abandonment. I know Hephaestus didn't teach you how to wield fire against another like that. And pray tell, which of the Anemoi taught you how to summon the winds? Hmmm? What's wrong with you?"

Artemis' eyes filled with tears as her father brought her down to size. She'd only wanted to teach Deivos a lesson, to put him in his rightful place. She wouldn't have hurt him that much. She would have exerted her power over him just enough to make him understand that her wish was his command. Her orders were meant to be followed. Yet her father had conveniently thwarted her plans.

"I . . ."

"You what?"

"I only meant to scare him," she said, blinking rapidly to keep her tears from falling.

Zeus approached her, and clasped her hands in his. His stern expression softened as he gazed into her eyes. "You've my temperament, dearest. I was just as rash at your age, but you need to curb those impulses. We are gods and goddesses, and are meant to rule over mortals. Yes, we have our own feuds amongst family here, but we do not hurt each other the way you've tried to hurt Deivos. Poseidon would take offense to your hurtin' his offspring. I know I would."

"But –"

"Can it, Lovely. I don't want to hear it. Whatever you did to dampen my nephew's abilities, I suggest you refrain from doin' so again. To anyone. I created you, Artemis. I can take your life without thinkin' twice. We are mighty, but we can still fall. Remember 'at when you try to hurt someone in the future."

He disappeared without another word, leaving her

alone in the middle of her courtyard. Puddles of water surrounded her, and her clothes were stuck to her skin. Yet she took no notice of any of it. Her mind reeled with the lecture her father had given her. He'd put her in her place, though he had no clue as to what she planned for him.

She bristled with anger at the fact that he'd threatened to take her life if she stepped out of bounds once more. Deep inside, she knew she wouldn't let him. She loved her life, as well as every aspect of what being the *Goddess of the Hunt* entailed. She would not let her father take her livelihood from her. Nor would she bend to his will or anyone else's. She had the right to live her life the way she wanted to live it. No one was going to take it from her. Not even Zeus.

CHAPTER 11

Artemis closed her eyes, and orbed herself back to her bedroom. She summoned her half-brother, Hermes, as she moved about the room. He appeared before her with his golden crown askew, and his chiton completely wrinkled. His severe disarray was appalling, as was the stench of sex that poured off of him. So much so, that she now regretted calling him forth.

His blue eyes were dilated, and spittle dripped down his chin. "You rang?" he quipped as he swayed back and forth.

"Yes, I did, but it looks like I've caught you at a bad time."

He laughed, and shook his head to clear it. "No, no.

I'm ok."

"Are you?" she asked as she took a step back to assess him.

He stumbled toward the chaise lounge in the upper left corner of the room, and dropped his five-foot-eleven frame onto it. "I'm fine. What's up?"

Artemis frowned, and chewed upon the tip of a fingernail. "I was hoping you could assist me, but I'm no longer sure if it's a good idea."

"Why not?"

"You're drunk."

"Psssh! This? I'm a god, Sis. I can warp myself out of a hangover."

She raised a brow in question. "Can you?"

He grinned. "Oh, yeah."

"Prove it."

His smiled disappeared. "What?"

"You heard me. Prove it."

Hermes' blue eyes focused on her face as he did his best to hold himself upright. Apparently, he hadn't expected her to call his bluff. His lips thinned to a tight line. Clutching the edge of the chair between his fingers, he closed his eyes, and began to concentrate. She took another step back as he began to glow.

A soft hum vibrated throughout the room as the glow surrounding Hermes grew stronger. Artemis had called his bluff, but she'd never expected him to act upon it. She'd thought he was kidding about his making the effects of his hangover dissipate. The hum intensified as the light completely enveloped her brother's bulky frame. A soft gasp escaped her as the tumescent glow shot outward. She closed her eyes to shield them from the unexpected luminescence.

Several minutes passed before the room returned to normal. She stood up straight, and opened her eyes to find a smug-looking Hermes sitting before her. The scent of alcohol and sex were gone, as were the effects of his inebriation. He sat in front of her, looking as good as new.

"Holy hell!" he breathed.

"What?"

"I never knew I could do that."

"Do what? Become the world's biggest fireball?"

He glared at her momentarily. "Get rid of a hangover. I lied, you know. But damn! That fucking rocked!"

She chuckled softly, and shook her head. "I bet."

"So what did you want me for?"

She pulled a chair over to him, and promptly sat down. Settling the skirt of her dress across her knees, she said, "I need you to keep an eye on Zeus."

"Come again?"

"I said –"

He cut her off with a quick jerk of his head. "You want me to spy on Zeus?"

"Well, no."

"But you just said . . ."

"That I want you to keep an eye on Zeus."

"That's spying."

"No, it's not."

"Yes, it is!" he balked.

She clenched her hands into tight fists. It dawned on her that she'd misjudged him. Deep inside, she'd prayed that he'd give up on his allegiance to their father. That he'd help her with anything necessary. How wrong she'd been. Hermes would lay his sword at her father's feet if it meant he'd get ahead in the scheme of things.

"It's not exactly spying, per se," she stated, moments later.

He crossed his arms upon his chest, his eyes full of suspicion. "How so? What's Father done that requires such secrecy?"

"I . . . I don't know."

"You don't know?"

"Yes."

"So, let me get this straight. You want me to watch Dad's every move, but you can't tell me why?"

She nodded, keeping her face impassive. "Uh-huh."

His eyes widened as a light bulb went off inside his head. "It . . . Does this have to do with that picture Apollo showed me?"

The sound of her heart beating thundered loudly in her eardrums. "Sort of."

"Who is she?"

She shrugged nonchalantly. "I'm not sure."

"But . . . ?"

"All I know is that she's tied to us somehow."

"And?"

"Daddy knows. I'm sure of it."

"Is that why you want me to keep tabs on him?"

"Yes."

"What if your plans backfire?"

She smirked with amusement. "How would they?" she quipped. "You have no idea what they are."

"No, I don't," he agreed. "But you're known as the chaste huntress for a reason, Artemis. You're up to something. Whatever it is, I want in."

"Do you?"

He tilted his head at her in acknowledgment. "Aye."

A smile tugged at the corners of her mouth. The fact that he wanted to help her was unexpected, but welcome. With his trailing their father's every move, they'd glean the needed information from Zeus in no time. Hermes' involvement in her plans would work out to her advantage in more ways than one.

She clapped her hands with delight. "Perfect!"

He snorted with amusement. "Aren't you going to tell me what your plans are?"

"In due time, yes."

"I see. What now, then?"

"Now," she said as she pushed herself to her feet, and stared down at him, "you get to watch Zeus carefully. If he notices something, or questions you for any reason, you can claim your innocence in not knowing what I'm up to."

"How's that going to work? Zeus isn't stupid."

"I know he's not. The less you know right now, brother, the better."

"What if – ?"

She cut him off with a quick flick of her hand. "I think we're done for now. How about you head to Daddy's house, and see what's going on there?"

His mouth pursed with displeasure. "Is that your wish?"

"Yes."

"Very well," he said, and disappeared with a resounding pop that echoed off of the room's walls.

CHAPTER 12

Artemis stared at the chaise lounge Hermes had occupied moments ago with bewilderment. She hadn't expected him to agree to things so easily. Never-the-less, she was pleased that he had. It would make things easier in the long run. The fact that she hadn't shared her plans with him would ensure that no one would be privy to them from get-go. Aside from Apollo, of course.

A sigh of frustration escaped her as she gazed at her surroundings. She'd expected Nephele to return with Apollo's reply in no time at all, yet she was nowhere in sight. She supposed it was because Apollo still inhabited his place amongst the blue skies, but it honestly didn't take so long to deliver a wretched letter.

Cracking her knuckles with impatience, she strode toward the door of her bedroom, yanked it open, and shouted down the hall for another attendant. Iokaste and Amynta, two of her handmaidens appeared, moments later. Flustered, they catered to her demands, and set about in preparing another bath for her. Artemis watched as they moved about the room, speaking amongst themselves as they finished putting everything together.

Standing near the bathtub, the women waited for further instructions. Artemis stood, and walked in their direction, calmly waiting for them to help her undress. They stepped forward, and quickly divested her of her garments. She smiled, and thanked them before slipping into the porcelain tub. She then dismissed them with a flick of her hand.

Her body sank into the warm water as the door latched closed behind them. She allowed herself to relax, enjoying the warmth that now covered her every limb. The scent of roses, jasmine, and gardenia wafting into the air soothed her frazzled nerves. The last few days – heck, weeks, had taken their toll on her, and she was beginning to feel the weariness spreading throughout her entire body.

She enjoyed these moments of respite, as they allowed her to make better sense of the world she lived in. Granted, life as a goddess was hectic, at best. There was always something, or someone, drawing her attention. Mortals, most of all, sought her out whenever possible, entreating her to a multitude of requests they hoped she'd help them with. They lived for the blessings she bestowed upon them, while she, in turn, basked in their adoration.

She loved her life, and wouldn't change things for the world. Yet there were times she wanted more. She hated living in other people's shadows, most especially her father's. Zeus ruled Mount Olympus as he saw fit, and dished out punishments accordingly. If something wasn't to his liking, he changed the circumstances until they suited him in every way. He was the king, and every god and goddess knew it. They followed his every rule to the letter, though everyone knew there were a good many things they could get away with before Zeus demanded order.

Artemis wanted that power. She wanted her family and friends to revere her, to lay their glory at her feet. She dreamed of the moment when she didn't have to answer to anyone but herself. The thought of living under her father's rule annoyed her, as did the restrictions he imposed on her and the rest of the pantheon.

She aimed to change things once she achieved her ultimate goal. Zeus would not be happy, she knew. He loved the power he exerted over her and the rest of her peers. She planned to put Hera in her place as well. That woman had far too much power. Power, she realized, she could use to her advantage.

Settling back against the edge of the tub, Artemis smiled as she thought about the changes she'd put into motion soon enough. She didn't care that she was being selfish. For once, she was thinking about herself and no one else. There would be opposition, she knew, but she would meet it head-on when the time came. She'd reap the fruits of her labor in more ways than one. Of that, she was sure.

CHAPTER 13

Artemis sat up abruptly as a cold mist surrounded her. Some of the now lukewarm water spilled to the floor. Wrapping her arms around her upper body, her eyes widened with horror as she watched the walls of her home dissolve. The cream-colored walls were soon replaced with an aqua-colored marble. Her heart hammered within her chest as she realized she was now in her uncle's domain.

A door opened to her left, and Poseidon himself strode into the room. She slipped lower into the water, keeping her arms wrapped around her heaving bosom. Her uncle stared down at her, his stormy blue eyes dark with an emotion she could not identify.

"Uncle!" she said.

The corners of Poseidon's mouth twitched with amusement. "Artemis," he replied as he snapped his fingers in front of him.

A chair materialized in thin air, and gently floated to the floor. He sat down, and crossed one leg upon the other. The door swung open, and a slew of servants hurried inside. They set about in preparing a table Artemis hadn't taken notice of when she'd appeared in her uncle's quarters. They spoke softly amongst themselves, sending covert glances in her direction as they worked.

Her face flushed with color as she realized what they must have been thinking. She was naked, and sitting in a tub full of water in front of Poseidon. To them, it didn't matter that they were family. All they saw was a man and a woman in what looked like a compromising position. It didn't matter that things between them were completely innocent.

She frowned, and turned her attention back to Poseidon. "What am I doing here?"

"We need to talk."

"You could have come to Mount Olympus."

He rolled his eyes, and shook his head, several blond locks falling across his brow. He cleared his throat, and dismissed his servants with a quick jerk of his head. They filed out of the room in a single line, the door swinging softly closed behind them.

"I prefer to conduct business here, away from my brother's prying eyes."

"You fear Zeus?"

"Who doesn't? I don't exactly fear him, per se. I like my privacy, that's all. This," he waved his arms about, "suits my purposes perfectly."

Goosebumps erupted all over her flesh as she became cognizant of the rapidly cooling water. "You could have sent word, Uncle. I'd have come better prepared."

"Where's the fun in that?"

He pushed himself to his feet, and walked toward the massive bed to the right of him. He picked up a white sheer garment, admiring the fabric with appreciation. A knowing smile played across his lips as he set it down once more.

"Why don't you get dressed?"

"With what? My things are back on Mount

Olympus."

He pointed to the articles of clothing lying on the bed. "These are for you."

"But . . ."

"How did I know?"

"Yes."

He walked over to her, and knelt beside the bathtub. He dipped a finger into the cooling water, and smiled. "I am the ruler of the seas, Artemis. The water belongs to me. I know everything and everyone who sets foot in it, be it on land or sea. I'm always aware when you or any of my brethren partake of such cleansing rituals."

"But you've never . . ."

"Overstepped my boundaries?" She nodded. "I've never had to. This time, however, was a necessity. You and I have some unfinished business."

"Can I at least get some privacy?"

He stood up, and took a step back. "Of course."

Her frown deepened. "Can you leave?"

"I think not, but I will accord you the privacy you so desire." A thick terry towel appeared in his hands. He gently placed it across the tub's edge, and turned his back on her. "You may proceed."

Growling with frustration, she grabbed the towel, and promptly stood up. Rivulets of water cascaded off of her skin in every direction. She wrapped the thick cloth around her slender frame, and stepped out of the tub. She marched toward her uncle's bed, and stared at the clothing he'd assembled for her. The sheer fabric of the dress was not something she usually wore. Unfortunately, there was nothing else for her to wear. Granted, she could have summoned something more appropriate, but she had a feeling it wouldn't be to Poseidon's liking.

With a sigh of discontent sliding past her lips, she allowed the towel to drop to the floor. She could feel her uncle's eyes pinned on her back as she moved forward to dress. Grabbing the thin silk undergarments, she slipped her legs into them, and promptly pulled them up. She fastened the white brassiere across her breasts, and slid the dress over her head. A pair of golden sandals appeared on her dainty feet.

She turned around to face Poseidon. "Well?"

He smiled, and whistled with appreciation. "Beautiful." He held out his hand, and waited for her to take it. "Shall we?"

She stared at his extended appendage. "What?"

He inclined his head toward the table laden with all sorts of fruits, cheeses, meats, drinks, and a myriad of assorted dishes. "I've had dinner prepared for you."

She raised a brow in question. "Have you been watching me?"

His smiled broadened. "Perhaps." He led her toward the table, and drew out a chair for her.

She sat down, and gingerly smoothed the dress's skirt around her knees. "Thanks," she said as he made his way to the other side of the table, and sat down.

Artemis broodingly stared at her uncle, trying to make sense of the current turn of events. She could not fathom as to why he'd brought her to Aegae. There was nothing of importance for them to discuss. Granted, she'd mentioned the *Child of Calamity* to him not too long ago, but she hadn't revealed too much about what she knew of the girl to him. Had she?

Poseidon cleared his throat, and drew her attention to him. "You're wondering as to why I've brought you here."

"Yes."

"Do you recall our previous conversation?"

"The one in the gardens back home?"

"That's the one."

"What about it?"

He reached out, and grabbed a plate, promptly filling it with several fruits, cheeses, and rolled meats. His eyes bored into her as he plucked a grape, and shoved it between his lips. "I believe you required a favor in exchange for telling me what you know about the *Child of Calamity*."

"I remember that, yes."

He leaned forward in his chair, the look on his face unreadable. "I did a little digging of my own."

Her pulse thundered in her ears. "And?"

He snapped his fingers, and a piece of paper materialized nearby. Her mouth grew dry as she watched it flutter to the table in front of her. She gazed at the very picture she'd shown Apollo several days ago.

"You recognize it."

"Yes."

"Who is she?"

She looked at him, perplexed. "You don't know?"

"I'd like you to tell me."

"Uncle . . ."

He crossed his arms upon the table's edge. "What do

you want her for?"

"N – No reason."

His eyes narrowed. "You're lying."

"Am I?"

"You never do things without having a solid reason, Artemis. Why does this woman intrigue you so? She's nothing. She's not even one of us."

She snapped out of her stupor, and sat up straight. "How do you know?"

"I just do."

"But you don't," she said, amused. "That's why you're plugging me for answers."

His face blanched. He hadn't expected her to catch on so quickly. "Perhaps," he murmured, deftly pulling himself together. "Why do you believe she's the *Child of Calamity*?"

She shrugged nonchalantly. "Instincts. She's tied to us. I know she is."

He leaned back against his chair. "That's all you have to go on? Your gut's feelings?"

She pushed herself to her feet, angrily staring down at Poseidon. "Maybe, but it's all I've got right now."

"You know who she is, don't you?"

"Maybe. I've a feeling you already know, Uncle, which means you never needed to see me in the first place."

He snorted with amusement. "Clever girl."

"What do you want?"

"Whatever you're up to, I want to know. I'd like to assist you."

"Do you?"

"Yes."

Her hackles rose, and her eyes narrowed. "I'll think about it, and get back to you on that, Uncle," she said, and promptly orbed herself home.

CHAPTER 14

The scent of apple blossoms and gardenias assailed Artemis' nose as she reappeared in the middle of her garden. Tears coursed down her cheeks unbidden as she crumpled to the ground. The weight of what she'd set into motion lay heavy upon her shoulders.

In sharing her thoughts about the *Child of Calamity* with Apollo, she'd unleashed a giant can of worms. No one had known about the child's existence until she'd done so. Granted, the child was no longer a child, but rather a fetching nineteen-year-old young woman. One who drew a person's attention everywhere she went. The girl was mortal, but she also possessed the blood of a very powerful god. In Artemis' mind, she belonged to Zeus.

Callidora exuded a power unlike any other, even if she wasn't yet aware of it.

Curling up into a tight ball, Artemis pulled her knees up against her chest, burying her face in the small dip between them. Her body shook as she cried, wishing that she could somehow change the course of some of the actions she'd undertaken, thus far. It upset her that far too many were now privy to Callidora's existence. Such circumstances did not bode well for her plans. She wasn't sure as to how she would be able to fix things.

Her tears subsided, moments later. Uncurling her legs, she lay on her side, and stared at the flowers dipping to and fro in the distance. A small smile spread across her lips as she felt Zephyrus' gentle touch, the *God of the West Wind*, ripple across the exposed flesh of her left shoulder. He materialized before her, his light brown hair blowing gently around his head. His amber eyes were full of kind understanding.

He leaned down, and clasped her hands, carefully pulling her to her feet. Guiding her over to the bench beneath her favorite willow tree, they sat down. He smiled softly, and brushed her tears aside with the pads of his thumbs before patting her hands in reassurance.

"My dearest Artemis," he murmured. "Yer in a pickle, aren't ye?"

She stared down at their intertwined hands as her face grew warm. "Somewhat."

"The winds know yer secrets, dear one."

She looked up, her eyes wide with horror. "My secrets?"

"Aye. Depending on which one of us blows across each new day, what we hear is nev'r the same. There are tales, Artemis, of the webs ye weave."

Her throat constricted as realization dawned on her. "How far and wide have the rumors gone?"

"Word has gone no further than what I and my brothers have discussed."

"But . . . ?"

"Ye must be careful," Zephyrus replied. "There are those who will not take kindly to what ye have set into motion."

"I know."

"No, dearest, ye don't. Word has a way of getting out. More will know."

She worried her lower lip in thought. "Meaning?"

"Be careful as to whom ye trust. There are wolves in

sheep's clothing."

"You speak in riddles, Zeph. Why?"

He grinned, though his mirth did not quite reach his eyes. "Because I must. I only came to warn ye. There's treachery afoot, and ye are in the thick of it."

She searched the depths of his eyes for a sign that he was lying. Yet she saw nothing that alluded to that fact. He was telling her the truth. Something, she knew, that came at a great cost. One she hoped he would never have to pay.

"Thank you," she breathed, squeezing his hand.

"Ye risk a good many things, child. I fear for ye."

"You needn't, Zeph. I'll be fine. I thank you and your brothers for guarding my secrets."

"We are good at such things. Ye would be surprised as to what we know about the entire pantheon."

She chuckled softly, and shook her head. "I can imagine."

Zephyrus pulled his hands free of hers, and stood up. His gentle look warmed her from within. "Company heads this way. I must go. Remember what I said, Artemis."

"I will," she said as her eyes closed of their own

volition.

She felt Zephyrus' light touch blow across her left cheek. He took the soft breeze with him as he said goodbye. Her eyes opened as she heard several clinks of metal rubbing together in the distance. Nephele appeared, moments later, a thin piece of parchment clutched between her fingers. She came to a stop in front of her, and promptly dropped to her knees. Her blond hair lay in subtle disarray around her shoulders.

"You have word from Apollo?" Artemis inquired.

Nephele looked up at her beloved mistress. "Yes."

"Let's hear it."

The girl extended the letter in her direction. She accepted the paper, and quickly broke the seal. She scanned the words hastily scrawled across the vellum's surface. A broad smile spread across her lips. Nephele witnessed her delight, though she had no idea as to what had brought it on.

"You may go."

Nephele stood, and executed a perfect curtsy in front of her. "Yes, Milady."

Artemis grabbed her arm as she turned to leave. A small brown bag appeared in the palm of her hand. "This is for the great service you have done for me."

Nephele's hazel eyes opened wide. "You're dismissing me?"

"No. Consider it a gift," Artemis replied. "I have need of you yet."

A sigh of relief escaped the girl's lips. "I . . . Thank you, Mistress."

"Please, call me Artemis."

Nephele swallowed past the lump now forming in her throat. She nodded with understanding, curtsied once more, and hurried out of the garden without a backward glance in Artemis' direction. The goddess chuckled to herself, and shook her head. She reread her brother's note before setting it on fire. The ashes scattered to the winds, taking with them Apollo's words.

Pushing herself to her feet, she breathed a sigh of relief. Zephyrus' word had calmed her down considerably. She was able to make sense of the precariousness of her current situation. Though others were now cognizant of the *Child of Calamity's* existence, they had no idea as to who she really was, whereas she and Deivos did. She suspected that Hades also knew of the girl's true origins, but he would never divulge that information. He had his own cards in which to play.

Never-the-less, she had enough information to go on when it came to Callidora Spiros. She'd use it to her advantage. The changes she would instigate were intended to better the state in which the pantheon currently found itself in. With Apollo and Hermes' help, she'd take Mount Olympus as her own. It was her due, after all.

Taking one last look at her surroundings, Artemis closed her eyes, and fled the confines of her home. Her heart raced as she anticipated seeing her beloved brother. She couldn't wait to put into motion the rest of her plans. Somehow, some way, everything would come together, and she'd finally make her dreams come true.

CHAPTER 15

"You rang?" Apollo whispered into Artemis' ear as he materialized behind her.

A knowing smile played about her lips as she clutched the Battery Park boardwalk railing. Her eyes raked the horizon. Liberty Island and Ellis Island loomed in the distance. The moment was peaceful, one she enjoyed immensely. Yet she knew the contentment she was feeling would not last long.

She turned around to face her brother, taking in his swollen cheeks and haggard appearance. "What took you long enough?"

He avoided her intense scrutiny, shuffling from foot to foot. "Yeah, umm . . . I was detained."

Her hackles rose, as did her suspicion. "By whom?"

"No one of importance."

"Father summoned you?"

"No."

"Then who?"

He shrugged. "It's no one you need to worry about. At least, not yet."

Her silvery-yellow eyes widened with alarm. "What have you done?" she asked, her voice barely a whisper.

"H – Hera," Apollo stammered.

"You told her?"

"No, but she caught me trying to find out more about the girl whose picture you showed me. I recalled it from memory, and made a copy. Hera came to see me, cited something about the sun needing to rise as scheduled. She saw the photo, and demanded I tell her who she was. I said I didn't know, so her cronies tried to rough me up."

"Did you cave under the pressure?"

"No. I think that's what pissed her off more."

Artemis released a pent-up breath, nervously wringing her hands together. "So my plans . . . They're safe?"

Apollo nodded. "Yes, but I'm not sure for how long. Hera . . ."

"Hera will look into things, I know. This means we'll need to be more careful from now on."

"How? That woman can sniff things out from a mile away."

"Not this. Not if you keep quiet."

Apollo's shoulders slumped with defeat. "I don't know, Sis. I'm not good at that. At least, not for long."

Artemis approached him, and curled a hand beneath his chin. She gently tugged his head up so that they were looking at one another, eye to eye. "You are," she cooed. "You need better discipline, that's all. This will be a good lesson in learning how to do just that."

He pulled his chin out of her grasp, and ran a hand through his blond hair. "I can never understand your faith in me."

"You're my twin, brother. I'm obligated to have faith in you," she said, chewing on her lower lip in thought. "There is a way to redeem yourself, however."

"How so?"

"Keep an eye on the girl for me."

"How am I going to do that?"

She glared at him, and turned around to face the turbulent waters of the harbor once more. "You're the *God of Light.* You rule the skies as you see fit, as well as see and hear everything below you. Keeping an eye on her will be as easy as making a pie."

He came to stand beside her, his eyes roving over the stormy seas. "What do I get in return?"

A knowing smile played about her lips as she glanced at him out of the corner of her eye. "Me."

"Is that a promise?"

"Yes."

"Then you have a deal."

He dematerialized without uttering another word, leaving her alone to enjoy the beautiful scenery spreading out before her. A soft sigh escaped her lips as she leaned against the railing. So far, things weren't going as planned, but she had faith that they would in the long run.

She'd have the *Child of Calamity* in the palm of her hand soon enough. The prospect pleased her immensely, more than she thought it would. Mount Olympus would be hers. She'd make sure of that, no matter the cost.

Taking a deep breath, she took one last look at the harbor in front of her, and orbed herself home. There was time enough yet to put the rest of her plans into order. For now, she would kick back, relax, and enjoy the ride for all it was worth.

ABOUT THE AUTHOR

Lissette E. Manning is an author from Connecticut. She has been writing since she was six-years-old, and enjoys giving life to the stories always brewing in her head. She enjoys reading, music, playing video games, spending time with friends and family, and is also a bit of a computer geek.

Connect with her online:

Email: lizziebeth1095@sbcglobal.net

Facebook: http://www.facebook.com/LissetteElizabethManning

Twitter: http://www.twitter.com/xLizzieBethx

Website: http://www.simplistik.org

Blog: http://www.simplistik.org/lissetteemanning

PInterest: http://pinterest.com/gethsemane95

Goodreads:
http://www.goodreads.com/author/show/4867044.Lissette_E_Manning

Proof

22720749R00063

Made in the USA
Charleston, SC
28 September 2013